PETUNIA

by Roger Duvoisin

Alfred A. Knopf

New York

In the meadow, early one morning, Petunia, the silly goose, went strolling. She ate a bug here, clipped off a clover leaf there, and she picked at the dewdrops on the goldenrod leaves.

Then, suddenly, she saw something
she had never seen before in the
meadow. What was it?

Petunia stole closer and closer
and sniffed at it from all sides.

"By Goosey Gander," she said, "it does not
smell like food for a goose. But I believe I
have seen such a thing before. . . ."

"Yes, I have seen one under Bill's arm when he came out of school. It's a Book. That's it. A BOOK!

"Come to think of it, just the other day I heard Mr. Pumpkin telling Bill that Books are very precious. 'He who owns Books and loves them is wise.' That is what he said.

She slept with it . . .

she swam with it.

And, knowing that she was so wise, Petunia also became proud,

and prouder

and prouder . . .

so proud

that her neck stretched out several notches.

"He who owns Books and loves them is wise," repeated Petunia to herself. And she thought as hard and as long as she could. "Well, then," she said at last, "if I take this Book with me, and love it, I will be wise too. And no one will call me a silly goose ever again."

So Petunia picked up the Book, and off she went with it.

And so, wise Petunia built a fire in the other end of the hole and fanned it well with the Book.

Her trick worked nicely. Noisy, choking with smoke, jerked his head out of the hole and ran off howling with pain. His nose was singed with the fire, and his ears were cut and bruised.

Poor moaning dog.

But Petunia had other things to do.

Beside the hedgerow she met Straw, the horse, who was in pain from a toothache.

"Petunia," groaned Straw, "I'm dying. Surely, with your wisdom, you can stop this horrible pain."

"Glad to help," said Petunia. "Open your mouth. Why . . . you poor Straw . . . all these teeth! No wonder you have a toothache.

"Look at me. Do I have teeth? Of course not. So I have no toothache. I am going to stop that pain right now. I am going to pull *all* those teeth out. *All* of them. Let me get some pliers . . ."

But Straw would not wait for the pliers. He was so afraid to lose his teeth that he never talked of his toothache to another soul. He suffered in silence.

Poor forlorn horse.

But Petunia had other things to do.

Cotton, the kitten, went up the tree but could not come down. While he miaowed and miaowed, his friends called for Petunia.

"Glad to help," said Petunia. "I know just what to do. Since none of you is tall enough to reach Cotton, all of you will do it together. Donkey on top of Clover, Pig on top of Donkey, and so on up. Simple."

So Donkey climbed on top of Clover;

Pig on top of Donkey;

Goat on top of Pig;

Sheep on top of Goat;

Piggy on top of Sheep;

Turkey on top of Piggy;

Duck on top of Turkey;

Hen on top of Duck. . . .

Suddenly Clover cried out,

"Stop! My legs feel wobbly."

And she sat . . .

. . . and Donkey and the rest
fell into a heap, and
Cotton was so scared that
he fell on top of them.
They were all full of bumps.
   "Well," said Petunia, "Cotton
is *down*."
   So he was, poor bruised kitten.

But Petunia had other things to do. Getting prouder all the time, she felt her neck stretch further out.

She now wandered down the meadow, where she found some other friends gathered around a box.

"Ah, wise Petunia!" they shouted. "We found this box in the ditch beside the road. Maybe it's food, Petunia. Please tell us what the writing on it says."

"Glad to help," said Petunia. "Now, let's see . . . Why, CANDIES. That's what it says on that box. Yes, candies. You may eat them. Yes, of course."

No sooner had Petunia given the word than seven greedy
mouths tore up the box and grabbed the candies out of it,
and . . .

What a sight the animals were!

Some were burned.

Some were bruised.

Straw still suffered in silence.

Noisy still moaned.

Ida still worried about her chicks.

King still brooded over his comb.

All the barnyard was in trouble, and all because of Petunia.

Petunia's pride and wisdom had exploded with the firecrackers.

Her neck had shrunk back to its old size and was all bandaged up. She was the most downhearted of all, for she saw now that she was not a bit wise.

But suddenly Petunia spied the Book. The firecrackers had blown it open so that the pages showed. She had never seen them before. Now she saw that there was something written inside the Book which she could not read. So she sat down and thought and thought and thought, until at last she sighed, "Now I understand. It was not enough to carry wisdom under my wing. I must put it in my mind and in my heart. And to do that I must learn to read."

Petunia was filled with joy. At once she began to work so that one day she could be truly wise. Then she would help make her friends happy.